The Dragon Ate That Summer

Other Apple Paperbacks
you will enjoy:

The Ghost in the Noonday Sun
by Sid Fleischman

Oh, Brother
by Johnniece Marshall Wilson

Fourth Graders Don't Believe in Witches
by Terri Fields

School Daze
by Jerry Spinelli

The Dragon That Ate Summer

Brenda Seabrooke

AN
APPLE
PAPERBACK

SCHOLASTIC INC.
New York Toronto London Auckland Sydney

ISBN 0-590-46986-X

12 11 10 9 8 7 6 5 4 3 2 1   3 4 5 6 7 8/9

Printed in the U.S.A.   28

First Scholastic printing, May 1993

To Kevin — the keeper of dragons
To Kerria — the dog-powered skateboard driver

The Dragon That Ate Summer

Chapter One

. . . .

"I wish we had a hill," Alastair McKnight said as he tied his skateboard to Josh's. "Then we could really go fast."

"Yeah," Josh said. He tied his skateboard to Ricky's, and Sammy tied his to the end to make a train. . . .

"You'd think that a town named Hilliard would have at least one hill in it," Alastair said. He stuffed the piece of leftover rope into the pocket of his shorts. Alastair had great plans for the summer. The skateboard train was only the first one. Camp was next. Then there was the tree house he'd been designing all spring when he was supposed to be coloring maps. And then he wanted to work on a spaceship.

"All aboard!" Sammy shouted.

Alastair took off with a hard push on the lead board, but the train didn't follow the way he had planned. The skateboards didn't skim smoothly along the sidewalk. Instead, they bucked and buckled, veered and jerked. The boys jumped off.

"It's not going to work," Josh said. "I told you it wouldn't."

"It will," Alastair insisted.

"Look out!" Ricky yelled. "Here comes Gruesome!"

The Whipples' boxer, Gruesome, loped toward them. His tongue hung down almost to his knees as he grinned at them. He was always digging or climbing or jumping out of the Whipples' yard and racing over to Alastair's house to play.

"Come on, cut that out," Alastair said as Gruesome slurped his cheek. Gruesome thought he was a nine-year-old boy, too, like Alastair and his friends.

"Hey, I bet Gruesome could pull our train," Alastair said.

Gruesome wagged his stubby tail.

"He's real strong. Let's try it." Alastair tied the left-over rope to Gruesome's collar. The boys jumped on the train. Alastair picked up the rope. "Let's go, Gruesome."

Gruesome trotted down the sidewalk. The train followed smoothly the way Alastair had planned. Gruesome revved up to a run.

"Gruesome can really go!" Sammy yelled.

"This is better than a hill," Josh said.

"Yeah," Alastair said.

"We're flying!" Ricky shouted.

Houses and shrubbery flashed by. The warm summer air rushed by Alastair's face. But as the train neared the end of the block, a cat jumped off a porch and ran around the corner of a house. Gruesome swerved across the grass in pursuit of the cat, and the skateboard train rattled behind him.

"Whoa, Gruesome!" Alastair yelled, pulling on the rope rein. But Gruesome kept going.

Alastair heard the boys jump off behind him. He dropped Gruesome's rope just as the train hit a bump, but it was too late. Alastair's feet shot into the air. The rest of him followed, and then all of Alastair came down against a stop sign on the corner. There was a loud smack.

Oh no, Alastair thought as he lay against the curbing. His shoulder ached. His mother was going to be mad. And his plans for the summer were in trouble.

His mother was only a little exasperated after she realized that Alastair still had all his arms and legs and could walk. "I wish you would think before you do things," she said as she drove him to the hospital for X rays. "You know how Gruesome is about cats."

"I did think," Alastair protested. "I thought it would work."

"What happened?" Dr. Michaels asked as he examined Alastair.

"He was riding a dog-powered skateboard train," Mrs. McKnight said.

Dr. Michaels smiled. "We get all kinds of accidents, but this is a first."

The technician laughed as he wrote on a clipboard, "Fell off a dog-powered skateboard train" as cause of accident.

But Alastair didn't laugh when the doctor said his collarbone was broken. "Does this mean I can't go to camp?"

"That's right," Dr. Michaels said as he whistled "London Bridge is Falling Down."

Alastair didn't see what was so funny about his accident. Dr. Michaels seemed to be enjoying the whole thing. The technician laughed. Even his mother was smiling. Everybody was having a good time. Everybody but Alastair. His plans were ruined.

But then Dr. Michaels said, "A skateboard train, *hmmm.* I broke my arm in a goat-powered wagon when

I was nine. I missed camp that summer, too. It was tough. But it will be over before you know it."

Grown-ups always say that, Alastair thought. Still, he felt better. But what was he going to do for the rest of the summer?

Chapter Two

· · · · · · · · · · · · · · · · · · ·

"Please, Mom, let me go outside. Just for a little while,"
Alastair begged. Three days after the accident, he was
miserable. His mother wouldn't let him do anything
more exciting than turn the page of a book or run the
channel-changer around the TV stations. She wouldn't
even let him play video games because she said he
might get excited and jump around.

"No, Alastair, you have to stay quiet for your collarbone to mend. Too much exertion could jar it
loose."

Alastair got down on all threes with his fourth in a
sling and pretended to be a dog begging. "I need fresh
air," he panted. "I'm getting pale and sickly from stay-

ing inside. And soooooo bored. I've read until my eyes are about to fall out of my head and watched reruns on TV until I'm cross-eyed."

She relented with a laugh. "All right. But only in our yard. I don't want you running around with Gruesome. Dr. Michaels said for you to stay quiet."

"I'll be quiet," Alastair promised. He walked slowly through the door. The fresh air was like a tonic. He felt better already. It was great to be outside again. He headed for the shade of the oak tree beside his house.

Now he knew what an egg roll felt like, he thought as he carefully stretched himself on the lounge chair. His right arm was strapped to his chest with a kind of a sling around it. He was so bandaged and tucked that he could hardly move, even if he wanted to—which he didn't, because his collarbone ached too much. Only his hand was free. His summer was ruined, and his friends didn't even care.

Josh hadn't been hurt at all. Ricky and Sammy had skinned their knees and elbows. They'd complained so much, you'd have thought they were the ones with the broken bones, Alastair thought.

Now they had all gone to camp with the rest of Alastair's friends. He was the one who had to stay home and suffer. He was the one who couldn't do anything more strenuous than turn the pages of a book. He was the one all tied up in straps. He was the one who was going to be miserable all summer.

Alastair had a good view of the street in front where some men were working on the road. They were putting in a new sewer system, his father had said. They'd been working for several days, but Alastair hadn't been interested before his accident. Now watching the road machines was better than TV.

Mr. Hobson came out of his house next door. His shapeless face sort of melted into his neck without stopping for a chin. A thin black mustache curved into two little smiles above his mouth that only smiled when he thought he had caught Alastair doing something he shouldn't be doing.

He stood in his yard and watched the machines, too. Then he noticed Alastair. "Those machines are making too much dust," he complained. "They're ruining my flowers."

Alastair thought the red dust was probably good for plants. But Mr. Hobson was always fussing about his garden. He was a train conductor and only worked several days a week. The rest of the time he spent working in his garden. Alastair and his friends didn't dare step on Mr. Hobson's grass or take a shortcut through his hedge. They might dent something or bend a twig.

"What happened to you?" Mr. Hobson asked, nodding at Alastair's sling.

Alastair told him.

Mr. Hobson snorted. "That dog is a menace," he said without a word of sympathy for Alastair and went back in his house.

Alastair watched the men working in the street.

The machines droned and snorted. The backhoe dug and backed, dug and backed, like a giant monster eating the earth. Alastair began counting the times the backhoe bit into the dirt. He didn't have anything else to do.

He hoped his friends were having a miserable time at camp. He hoped they were attacked by giant mosquitoes. He hoped the food was terrible. He hoped the lake had dried up and that it rained every day so they couldn't go swimming or canoeing or any of the things he wished he were doing.

Wishing misery on his friends made Alastair feel better for a minute, so he did it some more.

He hoped there was a snake in the toilet, frogs in their bunks, bats in their hair. He warmed to his subject, and just when he got ready for a real gross-out with worms and stuff his mother interrupted.

"Alastair, where are you?"

His mother was checking on him to make sure he

17

wasn't doing something that might crack his collarbone again. Something like having fun.

"I'm lying under the tree," he replied in a pitiful voice. Maybe she would feel sorry for him and send him to a movie.

But she only sent his sister Claudia out with a glass of lemonade and a vitamin pill.

"Here, pill. Mom says to take this vitamin." She put the glass and the pill on the table beside the chaise lounge Alastair was lying on. Then she stood and looked at him critically with her head on one side. She was wearing her blond hair in a ponytail this summer. Alastair thought her droopy bangs made her look like a dog. "Don't you have anything better to do than watch those machines?" she asked.

"No. Mom won't let me. Want to play Monopoly?" he asked hopefully. Monopoly with Claudia was better than nothing.

"I'm too busy," she said.

"You're always too busy," he said.

Claudia tossed her head. Her bangs went up in the air, then came down messier than before. "I have a lot to do to get ready for my slumber party next week," she said as she went back to the house.

"Actually, those machines aren't really machines," he yelled after her. "They're giant insects that have been trained to work. Those men are their handlers."

18

She turned at the door and gave him a look from under her bangs.

He bet she was busy. Her toenail polish probably needed changing. Or she had to make an urgent phone call to one of her phony friends about that dumb party. She was twelve and heavily into those things now. She never had time for anything that was fun.

Alastair took a swig of the lemonade. It was cold and tangy and sweet at the same time. He leaned back and looked up at the sky. It stretched over him, brilliant blue and endless without a cloud in it. Just like his summer and just as boring, he thought.

"Alastair, did you take your vitamin?" his mother reminded him from the house.

He picked up the pill. It was shaped like a football. A Sportsman vitamin pill for sports lovers. He threw it into the flower bed.

"*Yeep,*" went something in the petunias.

"Yes, ma'am, that old pill is long gone," Alastair told his mother.

Alastair thought about his friends. Two whole days had gone by without a word from any of them.

The machines in the street stopped. The backhoe rumbled off down the street. The men got in trucks and drove away, leaving behind orange cones to mark the unpaved work area.

Alastair felt sleepy in the sudden quiet. There was a

rustling in the petunias. He hoped it was a breeze coming up. He could use some excitement.

But nothing else moved. The big oak tree above him was as still as a picture.

Alastair heard another rustle. He turned his head to watch the petunias. Something was making them bob up and down. Then they were still.

Just as he was about to look for something else to watch, the petunias moved again.

Alastair got up to investigate. It might be a turtle. He hoped it was. He would paint a terrible face on it and put it in Claudia's room.

Just then a big ruffled pink petunia disappeared.

Chapter Three

"Alastair," his mother called. "I don't want you running around. You might jar your collarbone. Come inside now where I can keep an eye on you."

"I'm not running around, Mom, honest. I'm just walking around a little bit," Alastair protested. "Dr. Michaels said I should walk some. It's good for my circulation."

"It's too hot outside now," his mother said firmly. "You can take a walk later."

"In just a minute, Mom." Alastair dashed over to the petunia bed and peered into the dense tangle of leaves. But he didn't find anything. No turtle. No bird. No armadillo. Just petunias and they weren't moving. Maybe there had been a low breeze.

"Alastair, what are you doing?" His mother's voice sounded awfully close. He turned around. She was right behind him.

"March!" she ordered.

"All right, Warden, I'll go peacefully."

His mother laughed. "I know it's hard for you to be inactive. But it could be worse. You could be in a body cast in the hospital."

Alastair supposed that would be worse. He was glad he'd only cracked his collarbone. He went in the house and lay on the sofa, watching cartoons that got sillier the longer he watched. He wished he could work on a model. That was his usual entertainment when he was sick. But with only one working arm, that was out.

He turned the sound down on the TV and tried to guess what the people were saying. It was more fun that way. He could make up his own stories.

He was deep in a jungle cave looking for treasure when his mother came in with an angry look. "Alastair, what did you do with my petunias?"

"Petunias? I didn't do anything with your petunias."

"I saw you looking at them."

"I didn't touch your petunias," Alastair protested. "I was just looking at them. What's the matter with them?"

"They're gone," she said. "That's what's the matter with them."

"I didn't pick them," Alastair said quickly.

"You didn't pick them. I didn't. Claudia didn't. Then who did?"

"Dad, maybe?" Alastair offered.

"Your dad didn't pick them." His mother sounded exasperated again. "I want to know what happened to my petunias."

"I don't know," Alastair said. "I was here watching TV."

His mother threw her hands up. "I suppose it's a mystery."

Alastair got up from the sofa with as much of a bound as he could manage, trussed as he was, and said, "Ah ha! The Case of the Missing Petunias."

"Alastair, stop jumping around like that."

"I'm not jumping," he told her. "I'm bounding like Sherlock Holmes. There's a difference."

"Oh, I see," she said. "Where are you bounding to?"

"To the petunia bed. I'm going to look for clues."

"Just for a little while," she said. "And no more bounding around, OK? Think before you do things, Alastair."

"I always do, Mom," Alastair said. "I'm not going to shake anything loose. It hurts too much, for one thing. For another, I don't want to have to wear these straps a minute longer than I have to."

Alastair went outside. Earlier the petunia bed had

been filled with ruffled double petunias. Now there was not a blossom to be seen. The stalks with their pointy leaves ended without flower heads. Alastair squatted down and searched around the plants for clues. If the blossoms had fallen off the stems, they would still be on the ground.

But he couldn't find one blossom, not even a petal. He combed the stalks with one hand. In several places he discovered some strange scratches in the dirt. The scratches led to some bushes.

"Aha! A trail," Alastair said aloud.

He dropped to his knees to follow, but it was hard to crawl with one arm strapped to his chest. Alastair managed to do it as he tracked the scratches into the azalea bushes.

He couldn't imagine what kind of animal would make such a trail. Turtles didn't leave trails like this. Sea turtles, maybe, but this was far from the sea. Alastair ran through all the possibilities he could think of. A big bird with an injured wing. A cat dragging something. Some kind of burrowing animal. A snake, maybe.

The tracks looped through the bushes and disappeared at the edge of the lawn.

Alastair scanned the yard. The flowers and shrubbery were still. Hidden somewhere in them was an animal. Its two little eyes were at this very minute watching him. The back of Alastair's neck prickled.

Across the yard the daisies began to nod as if they were agreeing with him. And then, as he watched, their heads bent down one by one, pulled by some unseen force. The stems sprang back up minus their heads.

Alastair crept across the grass. Whatever it was didn't seem to notice his advance. The daisies went on bobbing and disappearing.

Alastair reached the end of the grass. He peered into the daisies, and there was the strangest little creature he'd ever seen. It had a smiley mouth with small sharp teeth, pointy ears, short legs with curly toes, and scales. It was so small it would almost fit in his hand.

It looked up at Alastair with round little eyes.

"*Zeep*," it said.

"*Zeep*," Alastair replied.

He didn't know what this strange creature was, but he knew that he was going to keep it.

Chapter Four

Alastair had never been allowed to have any pets but fish because his sister was allergic to animals. He had had a succession of goldfish, but they weren't any fun. All they ever did was go *glub glub glub* all the time. He'd had a couple of turtles and a frog that he'd raised from a tadpole until it got into Claudia's room once and she'd had a fit. But you couldn't hug a frog and you couldn't teach a turtle to do tricks.

Now Alastair had found the best pet in the world, and he didn't even know what it was. All he had to do was catch it. That was going to be hard with one hand strapped to his chest. But maybe the creature was tame. It hadn't run from him. It didn't seem to be afraid.

"*Zuck*," it said. It sat back on its haunches and watched him with round eyes.

"Hey, you're a cute little creature," Alastair said as he reached out to touch it. He hoped it didn't bite or anything.

"*Xeep*," it said without moving.

Alastair touched its head with one finger. It felt warm and smooth, not at all like any amphibian he'd ever touched, the frog he'd had or the grass snake his third-grade class had kept in a terrarium all last year.

He stroked the creature's head.

"*Xxxxxxxeeeeeeeeeeeep*," it sort of purred.

Alastair let his finger slide down the back of the creature's head where the scales were raised in a zigzag that went all the way down to its long tail and ended in a point like an arrowhead. Up and down his finger went, almost to the tail.

Alastair thought he could pick the creature up with one hand if it would let him.

"Will you let me pick you up, fella?"

"*Zhummmm*," it purred.

Alastair slipped his hand under its stomach and lifted. It was surprisingly heavy for such a small creature. Alastair supposed the scales made it heavier.

The creature snuggled into his lap. He thought it must never have seen a human before. That was probably the reason it wasn't afraid of Alastair. He scritched it under its chin. He would have to smuggle it into his room. Maybe if Claudia didn't know it was there, she wouldn't have an allergy attack.

But now he had to figure out how to do it. If he could leave the creature outside until dark, it would be easy to slip out while his mom and dad were watching TV and Claudia was on the phone or something. But if he put the creature down it might wander off or, worse, eat the rest of his mother's flowers and be discovered.

Alastair examined the sling that held his right arm. If he could slide the creature in on top of his arm, it would be hidden and he could carry it to his room without being seen. It might work.

He would have to try it.

"Come on, little fella, in you go." He slipped the creature into his sling. It fit perfectly after he got all of its tail crammed in. Only its nose peeked out. Alastair pushed it in a little farther. "Keep your nose in, fella," he told the creature.

"Zum hum," said the creature with a yawn. And then it was quiet.

Alastair stood up and crossed the lawn. He hoped his mother was busy. Maybe Claudia was on the phone. He opened the kitchen door.

"I was just about to call you," his mother said. She was around the corner in the breakfast area sitting at the table. He tried to sidle across the room so she wouldn't notice if his right arm sagged with the creature on it.

She frowned and stood up just as he reached the middle of the room. "Let me feel your head. You look a little flushed."

"I'm OK, Mom." He tried to turn away. He felt the creature wiggle. Maybe she wouldn't notice.

"Hold on, let me see." She put a hand to his brow. "You do feel warm."

Alastair ducked. "It's not easy being a detective in this heat, Mom," he said. "I think I'll go lie down."

He edged away. She was looking at him with suspicion. It was highly unusual for Alastair to lie down in the middle of the afternoon. But she let him go.

"Did you find my petunias?" she asked as he reached the door.

"No, but I'm still working on it."

Claudia was stretched across the hallway with her feet up on the wall. She was talking on the phone. As Alastair stepped over her, the creature wiggled again.

"What are you doing?" she said.

"I'm trying to go to my room."

"What's that you've got?"

"What?" Alastair tried to look innocent. His dark hair fell over one eye. He blew at it as though he were unconcerned.

"That thing you're carrying. What is it?"

"Nothing."

"A rat. You've got a rat."

"No, I don't."

"Mom, Alastair's got a rat."

"Why would I want a rat when I've got a sister?"

"Funny. I saw it move."

"It was only a muscle jumping." The creature moved again.

"There. You can't tell me that was a muscle. It's an animal."

"It's a muscle," Alastair insisted. He put his left hand over the opening of the sling where the creature was trying to poke its nose out. "I don't have anything but a broken collarbone and it hurts," he said pitifully. "Mom told me to go lie down."

He went past her to his room.

"Yeah, that was Alastair," he heard her say. "On the dog-powered skateboard train. He never thinks. The Whipples' dog, Gruesome, chased a cat and Alastair hit a stop sign. That was one time he did what the sign said." Then there were a lot of giggles.

He didn't know what was so funny about breaking your collarbone on a skateboard. In the safety of his room he put the creature on his bed and got a good look at it.

It looked like a dragon.

Chapter Five

"You can't be a dragon," Alastair said to the creature as it looked up at him with its big round eyes. "There's no such thing as a dragon outside of fairy tales."

He set it on the floor. He kicked off his shoes and sat down beside it. It still looked like a dragon. Although it was smaller than a cat, it had all the elements of a dragon: scales, claws, zigzag mane. But it couldn't be a dragon. "There's no such thing," Alastair told the creature again.

But it was a dragon. There was no other explanation. "You must be a baby dragon," Alastair said.

"Greep greep." The little dragon seemed to agree with him. It ambled over to his feet and began to nibble on his bare toes.

"Don't do that, fella, that tickles." Alastair pushed the creature away.

"HEEP HEEP," the dragon said loudly as it went back to nibbling.

Alastair remembered the pink petunias. "You think my toes are flowers and you're hungry." Alastair pushed the dragon away again and quickly slid his feet into sneakers.

The dragon nosed his sneakers. It backed away in such a hurry that it fell over. Alastair laughed. His mother was always telling him to put his sneakers in the wash so they wouldn't smell up his room.

He put the dragon in a shoe box in his closet and went to the kitchen to find something to feed his new pet. He had no idea what dragons ate. In books they were always eating people. Since this one liked flowers, he thought it might not be the people-eating kind. It was probably more of the vegetarian kind.

No one was in the kitchen when Alastair went to the refrigerator. He opened it and looked on the shelves for dragon food. There were several bowls of leftovers: tuna salad, rice, broccoli casserole, beef stew. He decided to try a little of everything. He picked up the bowl of broccoli.

"What are you doing?" Claudia's voice demanded behind him as he was taking the broccoli out.

Alastair jumped and almost dropped the bowl. He

must be getting careless if Claudia could sneak up on him without his hearing her.

"I'm getting a snack," he said.

She looked at the broccoli. "Since when did you start snacking on broccoli?"

"That's not all I'm getting. But as it happens, I like cold broccoli," he told her. "It's especially good when mixed with leftover tuna."

"I have to see this," she said as she folded her arms and leaned against the pantry door. She grinned and showed her braces.

Oh no, he groaned to himself. He was going to have to eat the broccoli. Maybe if he took a long time, she would leave. He put the bowls on the counter. The broccoli was awfully green. Then he went back to the refrigerator and took out the bowl of tuna. He got a plate from the cabinet. Then he got out a glass.

"What's that for?" Claudia asked.

"Milk. I'm thirsty."

He got the milk from the refrigerator and filled the glass.

"You sure are slow," she said.

"It takes longer when you can only use one hand," he reminded her.

He picked up the milk and started to drink.

"This could take all day," she said.

"Nobody asked you to watch. I thought your time

was too valuable to waste on your poor injured brother you wouldn't play Monopoly with."

"I'll play Monopoly with you now," she said.

Now Alastair had a real problem. If he refused she would get suspicious. But the dragon was hungry. What would it do without food for the hours a Monopoly game would take?

He took another sip of milk. He was stalling. His mind raced furiously.

"Um, I don't feel like playing Monopoly," he began.

"You've been begging me to play ever since the accident," she said. She squinted her eyes at him. He could see suspicion in them like tiny seeds getting ready to grow and bloom all over her face.

"I feel like playing checkers," he said.

Claudia opened her eyes back to normal size. "OK," she said. "I'll play a few games with you."

She went to the game cabinet in the den while Alastair put the broccoli back in the refrigerator. For a minute he'd thought he was going to have to eat the stuff himself.

His plan was to let her win so she would get bored soon and quit playing. But he couldn't let her win easily.

"Red or black?" she asked.

"Red." She liked the black.

Alastair won the first game. He hadn't meant to. It

had just happened. Maybe she had been letting him win.

In the next game he pretended not to see her far left checker sneaking across the board.

"Crown me!" she said.

"How'd you do that?"

Alastair thought he should get an Oscar for his performance. He let her win two games in a row, then a third. Now she was suspicious again.

"This is too easy," she said. Her eyes had that squinty look again.

"I'm getting tired," Alastair said. "Could we play again later?"

"Sure. Would you like to borrow my new magazines?"

"Any comics?"

"No." She tossed her ponytail. "I'm too old for comics. I have *Sixteen* and *Ms. Teen.*"

"Um, no thanks." Alastair knew he would never get too old for comics. He leaned back on the sofa. He hoped the dragon hadn't eaten its way out of the box in the closet. His shoes were in there. What would he tell his mother if the dragon ate his shoes?

········

Chapter Six

········

When Claudia finally went to her room, Alastair leaped up and went back to the kitchen. He got an apple and a celery stalk out of the refrigerator drawer. He put rice and broccoli on a plate. He poured milk into a cup so he could carry it in his right hand and took the food back to his room.

The dragon was whimpering and butting its head against the sides of the box when Alastair opened the door. "Poor little guy, don't be scared. I didn't leave you. I only went to get you something to eat." He set the plate on the floor and put the dragon in front of it.

The dragon sniffed all the food, then it picked up the celery stalk and began munching. It sat back and held the stalk with its front legs the way a squirrel eats a nut. Then it ate the apple the same way. It wrinkled its nose at the broccoli but ate it and then the rice, grain by grain.

"You must have been awfully hungry," Alastair said.

"*Fweep*," said the dragon.

Alastair poured some of the milk into the plate so the dragon could drink. It made slurpy noises as it lapped up the milk with its curly tongue. Alastair poured more milk until the dragon had drunk it all. Then it sat back and gave a loud burp.

There were sudden footsteps in the hall. Alastair listened for a second. His mother was coming. He scooped up the burping dragon and deposited it in his wastebasket. He put a comic book over the top, grabbed another and was sprawled across the floor, intent on reading when his mother opened the door.

She spied the plate and cup. "Alastair, you know you're not supposed to be eating in your room. There will be ants all over the place."

"No, there won't, Mom. I didn't drop a single crumb. Honest." Alastair felt safe saying that. The dragon had licked the plate clean.

"I came to tell you that I'm going to the store and I can stop by the library and get you some books if you'd like."

"OK."

"Any requests?"

Alastair thought for a minute. "I'd like some books about dragons if they have any."

"Dragons? Fiction or nonfiction?"

"Nonfiction."

His mother laughed. "Since dragons aren't real, all books about them would have to be fiction."

"I don't want stories," Alastair said.

"All right. I'll check with the librarian."

"Thanks, Mom."

"Do you feel all right?"

"Fine, Mom."

The minute the door closed, Alastair looked in the wastebasket.

The dragon was curled up sound asleep with its tail over its eyes. When Alastair picked it up to move it to a box in the closet, the dragon woke up and squirmed while making little squealing sounds. Alastair put it on the floor to see what it would do. He didn't know what to expect from this strange little pet. Who knew how dragons behaved, anyway?

As Alastair watched, the dragon ran around in small circles, still squealing like a baby pig. The circles got bigger until they took the dragon all the way to the closet door. On the next circle, the dragon went into the closet and Alastair heard a loud *ahhh* sound followed by a smell sort of like burning rubber mixed with perfume.

With dread in his heart, Alastair looked in his closet. The dragon had pooped in one of his new sneakers that he hadn't even worn yet because he had been saving them for camp. Why couldn't it have pooped in the old smelly one? The dragon was sitting beside the sneaker. It looked enormously relieved.

Alastair mentally kicked himself. Dragons weren't like fish and turtles and frogs. They were more like dogs and cats. He should have thought of that. Now his sneaker was ruined. He would have to try to clean it before his mother saw it. But first he put the dragon back in the shoe box and punched holes in the lid with a pencil. He put a rubber band around the box. "There. That ought to hold you until I get back. Now be quiet," he told the dragon.

A muffled *"Zeeeep"* came through the holes in the lid.

Alastair wrapped the sneaker in an old comic book. It smelled awful. He wished he could hold his nose but he had only one hand to carry the sneaker with. He wasn't going to stuff THAT into his sling.

He took it out to the backyard, where he hosed it down for a long time with the sprayer. He threw the comic book into the trash. It was one of his favorites, too—*Penguin Man Meets Action Ant.*

Alastair examined his dripping sneaker. It still smelled awful, and the inside was stained greenish-purplish-pinkish-yellow. He thought of all those petunias and the broccoli. El yucko!

His mother always soaked badly stained clothes in bleach mixed with water. Sometimes she even put his sneakers in to make them whiter. Alastair decided to try it. He didn't want to throw away his brand-new sneaker.

In the laundry room Alastair poured bleach into a pail. It didn't look like enough, so he added more. Then he put in water and dropped the sneaker in. He didn't know how long to leave it in. The stain was really bad and the smell was worse. Alastair decided to leave his sneaker to soak all night. He poured in a little more bleach. He wanted to be sure to get all the smell out of his sneaker.

Next he found a box for the dragon to use for a bathroom. That was what people did for cats. He didn't have any litter to put in the bottom. Dirt would be too dirty. He decided to use newspaper instead and tore yesterday's want-ad section into small pieces. He put the front page in the bottom and put the pieces over that. He hoped it would be absorbent enough. He also hoped the dragon would know what it was for. One thing Alastair was sure about: He wasn't going to feed the dragon any more broccoli.

······················

Chapter Seven

······················

"Dragons are fabulous monsters, bat-winged, fire-breathing, and scaly with barbed tails . . ." Alastair read. His mother had brought him three books about dragons and monsters from the library.

He examined his dragon. It had scales and a barbed tail but no wings, unless the little bumps behind its shoulders were supposed to grow into wings. He didn't see how that was possible. He felt the bumps. They were just bumps like little bunched muscles. His dragon didn't breathe fire either.

"Dragons are the embodiment of evil in mythic lore . . ." he read. Alastair looked at his dragon. It was playing with his shoelaces, more like a kitten than the embodiment of evil, whatever that was.

He read on. "Dragons are a symbol of good luck . . ."

Alastair looked up in confusion. How could dragons be evil and good luck at the same time? They must be one or the other.

Alastair turned back to the book. Some dragons live in the center of the earth, as keepers of the secrets of the universe, revealing them to the chosen. Other dragons serve as guardians of treasures. These creatures have a carbuncle or jewel between their eyes.

Alastair didn't know what a carbuncle was, but he didn't think his dragon had one. He decided that there must be a lot of different kinds of dragons. He was sure that his was one of the good kind. He checked its head. No jewel there.

In another book he read that dragons were symbols of strength and power. They were sharp-sighted and possessed healing powers. The book had a recipe for a cold cure that started off: "Steep seven silver scales of a dragon . . ."

Alastair discovered that dragons are grateful for favors and have huge appetites. He already knew the last without having to read it. His dragon was hungry all the time. But unlike the dragons in the books, his dragon was a vegetarian. It wouldn't touch the bits of leftover chicken he'd given it and made gagging sounds over the leftover beef stew.

"The recorded dragons that were slain by such famous

heroes as Roland, Beowulf, Siegfried, and Saint George were in reality lost dragons looking for a way back to their subterranean caves," Alastair read.

"Is that what happened to you, fella? Were you lost?"

"*Merrowpeep,*" purred the dragon. It rolled over on its back for Alastair to scratch its stomach.

"I don't think you know you're a dragon. You think you're a puppy or a kitten."

The little dragon rolled over again. It picked up Alastair's shoelace in its mouth and began to pull. "*Grrraup,*" it growled.

"You want to play tug-of-war. OK. But not with my sneaker." Alastair found a belt in a drawer. He flipped it around on the floor.

The dragon pounced on the belt and fastened its sharp little teeth on the end. It backed away, growling all the while. Alastair pulled the other way.

Suddenly the dragon let go of its end, leaped forward, and caught Alastair's end.

"So you cheat at tug-of-war." Alastair grabbed the other end.

The dragon growled ferociously.

"You're a tough little guy," Alastair said. "I think I'll call you Spike. Is that tough enough for you? Here, Spike." He snapped his fingers.

The dragon dropped the belt and ran on its short stubby legs to Alastair. It rubbed against Alastair's

43

knees, purring loudly. "You sound like a motorboat," Alastair said. "Not so loud. Claudia might hear you."

He scritched the dragon's ears.

Alastair thumbed through the books again, looking at the illustrations of dragons. None of them looked like Spike. None of them was roly-poly and cute, and they were all the wrong color. Spike was a sort of silvery blue. The book dragons were red, purple, dark green, and black and orange.

None of the books said a word about modern dragons, only about dragons of long ago. Alastair wondered why there weren't any books on dragons today. He decided to write a letter to his Uncle George. If anybody knew about dragons, Uncle George would.

It was lucky for Alastair that he was left-handed and that it was the right collarbone that was broken. He got out the notebook he'd used last year at school. It had a few blank pages left in the back. Alastair fished out an orange felt-tipped pen. He wrote:

> Dear Uncle George,
> This is from your nephew Alastair.
> How are you? I hope you are OK. I am OK except I broke my collarbone on a dog-powered skateboard and can't do anything. I cudden even go to camp.
> Do you know anything about modern drag-

ons? Mom got me some books from the liberry
but they are only about dragons from a long
time ago. I need to know right away.

Please write back in a hurry.

Yours truly,
Alastair

Alastair had a feeling some of his words weren't spelled right. He added a *t* to "cudden." It still didn't look right, but he thought Uncle George would understand. He could still read it. The important thing was to get the letter off as soon as possible so Uncle George would hurry and answer it.

He added, "P.S. It's a matter of life or death."

That should make Uncle George write back immediately. He addressed an envelope and went to find a stamp. He put his letter out in the box in front of the house for the mailman to pick up.

Uncle George knew all about strange things in the world. He was some kind of scientist. He worked at the Photon Institute, where they studied all kinds of monsters. Uncle George was always going to faraway places to track down monsters that had been seen or rumors of monsters. He'd been to Scotland to study Nessie, the Loch Ness monster, and to Tibet for the Abominable Snowman. He'd been to Oregon to study Bigfoot and to South Carolina to study the lizard man.

45

Alastair hoped his uncle was at the institute now and not off in the desert or on the ocean looking for sea monsters. Sometimes they didn't hear from Uncle George for months.

Alastair couldn't wait that long. He needed to know about dragons now.

Chapter Eight

Every day Alastair changed the dragon box. Spike only used it once a day, but that was more than enough for Alastair. If only he didn't have to pass Claudia's room on his way to the trash, it wouldn't be so difficult.

"What is that awful smell?" she screeched the next day as he was taking the box out to empty it.

"My sneakers," he mumbled, afraid that she would follow him.

At the trash can outside he ran into his mother. "What is that awful smell?" she asked.

"It was an experiment," he said wildly. He hoped she wouldn't ask what kind of experiment but, being his mother, she did.

"Um, I was trying to grow some mushrooms," he said. "But it didn't work."

"No, I can sense that," she said with a laugh. She didn't ask to see the experiment. There was something good about Spike's bathroom habit. It didn't invite careful inspection.

After that close call Alastair decided to use toilet paper instead of newspaper. He could get to the bathroom quickly and flush it away before the smell had time to fill the house. And he only had to cross the hall. He didn't have to pass Claudia's room. He still hated having to do it. It wasn't a perfect system, but it was the best Alastair could think of for now.

But later he almost got caught again when his mother found the sneaker in the laundry room. "Alastair, look at this sneaker. It looks like it is made of lace. What did you do?"

Alastair looked at his once-brand-new unworn sneaker. It did look like lace. There was hardly a spot that didn't have a hole in it. He'd forgotten and left it in the bleach water for several days.

"Um, I forgot, Mom. I'm sorry. I stepped in some dog poop and couldn't clean it. So I remembered that you always soak my sneakers in bleach."

"But not for weeks, Alastair." She sighed. "I wish you would think before you do things."

Alastair stopped himself from saying he did think, he just forgot. He should have remembered.

Every day he checked the mailbox to see if there was a letter for him. Two weeks went by without a letter from Uncle George or even a postcard from Josh. He had to find out more about dragons. One day as he walked back from the mailbox he saw Mr. Hobson.

Mr. Hobson bared his teeth in his version of a smile. Alastair didn't know if he was being friendly because of his broken collarbone or if he was laughing at him. But Mr. Hobson knew a lot about plants and gardens. They were natural things, sort of like dragons. Maybe he knew something about dragons as well. Alastair decided to ask.

"Dragons? Dragons!" Mr. Hobson echoed. "Well, I know about dragonflies but not much about dragons. They ate girls, didn't they? Maybe even little boys," he said with a sly look at Alastair. "Bad boys."

"Not all dragons ate people," Alastair said.

"Dragons are probably a lot like people," Mr. Hobson agreed. "Some were good and some were bad. But most were probably bad. Why else would all the old stories be about bad dragons?"

Alastair didn't know the answer to that. Maybe Uncle George did. "But where did they come from?" he asked. "And why aren't there any now?"

"They probably came from dinosaurs," said Mr. Hobson, "maybe a leftover dinosaur egg. They probably disappeared the way the dinosaurs did unless you count Komodo dragons as real dragons."

"Komodo dragons? I never heard of them," Alastair said. He could hardly contain his excitement. This might be the answer to the mystery of his dragon. But he couldn't let on to Mr. Hobson. He had to stay calm.

"Where do they live?"

"They live on the island of Komodo somewhere in Asia."

"Oh. Asia." There was no way Spike could have come from Asia. He was too small to have traveled that far.

Alastair made a list comparing Spike with the dragons of the stories.

Spike	Other Dragons
vegetarian	ate people and meat
loving	fierce
no wings	wings
little	giant
funny	scary
tiny claws	long claws
blue	red, green, orange, black

Alastair read over his list. It sounded like Spike wasn't even a real dragon because he was so different from the dragons of olden days. But he still looked like a dragon, and Alastair had no doubt that he was a dragon.

Chapter Nine

"Oh no! Not you!" Alastair heard Claudia say in the hall. He grabbed Spike off the floor and put him in the wastebasket. He threw a comic book on top. Then he flopped on his bed and pretended to be reading. He hoped Spike would go to sleep the way he had before.

"Hi," Josh said.

Alastair turned the page, pretending to read.

"It's me," Josh said.

"So what." Alastair was still mad at Josh for not writing.

"I'm back."

"So I see." Alastair turned a page.

"Don't you want to hear all about it?"

"All about what?"

"Camp. I'm back from camp."

"So what." Alastair turned another page.

"So we had a great time. Don't you want to hear about it?"

"You make it sound like you were in Outer Mongolia instead of at Ho Hum Hiawatha Lake."

"It's not ho hum. It's Hi Ho Hiawatha. It was fun. We went swimming and canoeing and horseback riding and hiking. I shot a bow and arrow."

"Anybody can do those things."

"You can't," Josh said.

"Maybe I did things that were more fun," Alastair said.

"You couldn't have. Nothing is more fun than camp." Josh sat down on the floor.

"Something is. And I did it." Alastair flipped over a page.

"What did you do? What?"

"I'm not going to tell you." Alastair didn't have to look at Josh. He knew Josh's curiosity was aroused. But he was trying to play it cool. Alastair knew the signs. The tips of his ears turned red when he was curious.

Josh said, "That's 'cause you didn't do anything."

"Yes, I did."

Josh sprawled across the floor. Alastair watched him

out of the corner of his eye. He was awfully close to the wastebasket. Spike hadn't made any noise yet. Alastair hoped he was asleep.

Just then there was a soft stirring sound from the wastebasket.

"You didn't even send me a postcard," Alastair said quickly to distract Josh's attention from the noise.

"Yes, I did," Josh said.

"Where is it, then?"

"I almost forgot." Josh pulled a postcard out of his back pocket. It was creased from being folded. "Here it is. I would've mailed it, but I didn't have a stamp." He held it out.

"They sell stamps at camps," Alastair said accusingly.

Josh grinned at the rhyme, but Alastair didn't. He didn't take the postcard either.

"Here." Josh tossed the card to him. Alastair waited a minute before picking it up.

"You promised to send me a card. Not bring it to me."

"I tried. Honest, I did. I didn't have time to go to the post office. It was way off away from everything."

"In two whole weeks you didn't have time to buy a stamp?"

"I told you. I was busy."

When Alastair still didn't pick up the card, Josh said, "Aren't you going to read it?"

54

Alastair reached for the card. It was a picture of a lake with a canoe paddled by two boys dressed like Indians in feathered headdresses. Alastair turned it over.

> Dear Alastair,
>   Camp is great. Wish you were here. Sorry about your axident. We went on a hike. I caught 3 fish. I'm learning to paddle a canoo.
> Your friend,
> Josh

They were interrupted by voices in the hall. "Mom! Please! You can't do this to me," Claudia was saying, her voice throbbing with drama.

His mother's voice was too low to hear as Alastair strained to listen. He didn't notice the faint scratching sounds in the wastebasket.

"But, Mom, it will be a disaster. My party will be ruined," Claudia wailed.

"No, it won't," said his mother in a louder voice. "I'll lay down the ground rules. The boys will stay out of your way."

The scratching noise became louder. Alastair heard it this time, but before he could do anything Claudia burst into his room.

"All right, you little monsters. If you cause any trouble tonight, I'll fix you." She glared down at them.

Alastair looked at Josh.

The scratching turned into a loud bump.

"What was that?" Claudia's eyes searched his room.

Alastair knew that Josh had heard it.

Bump.

The wastebasket moved.

Alastair saw Josh looking at the wastebasket. He must have seen it move. Now he would say something and Claudia would see Spike and then he would have to get rid of his pet dragon.

"What was that bump?" Claudia said again.

"You mean like that?" Josh kicked the wall with his foot.

"What do you mean we better not cause any trouble tonight? What's going to happen tonight?" Alastair tried to turn her attention away from the wastebasket.

"Tonight at my slumber party. You two better not pull any of your dumb tricks. No pie beds. No funny noises. No ghosts or things that go bump in the night. What are you doing in here anyway, practicing?"

She wasn't making sense. "Why do you think Josh is going to be here?" Alastair asked. He wasn't even friends with Josh anymore.

To Alastair's great relief, she forgot about the noise. She was too mad at the boys. "Because he's spending the night here. That's why." She stomped out and slammed the door.

"Is that true?" Alastair looked at Josh.

"Yeah. My parents have to go to a dinner over in Ashton. They won't be back until late. Your mom said I could spend the night here. She said we could catch up on the last two weeks."

Alastair looked away. How could he keep Spike's existence a secret from Josh with him here all night and the house full of girls, too? It was going to be a nightmare.

Chapter Ten

The wastebasket thumped again.

Alastair would never be able to keep Spike a secret from Josh now.

He would have to tell him. Josh was already looking at him funny. His eyes were almost crossed. Alastair knew Josh suspected something. He turned the problem over in his mind and made a decision. He would have to trust Josh. After all, he had covered for Alastair with Claudia.

He would have to tell Josh about his dragon. But first he would swear him to secrecy.

"If I tell you what I did this week, will you swear never to tell anyone no matter what?"

"I swear!" Josh crossed his heart and held up his right

hand. He had his "now-we're-getting-somewhere" look. His eyes were squinched into slits, his eyebrows were raised, and his mouth was stretched in a long straight smile.

But that wasn't enough for Alastair. This was a secret of such magnitude that it needed more than a simple "I swear." "You have to sign an oath," he told Josh.

"OK." Josh's ears were bright red all over now.

"In blood," Alastair said.

Josh paled under his camp tan but his ears stayed red. They seemed to quiver a little. "OK," he said a little less positively.

Alastair got his notebook out and after a minute's thought wrote the oath for Josh to sign.

> *I, Joshua Stone, do solemnly swear never to reveal to anyone a word about Alastair McKnight's secret. If I do, a horrible mummy's curse will befall me.*
>
> *signed*
> *Joshua Stone*

"Sign under your name," he directed. He found a pin for Josh to prick his thumb with.

"Can't I just use a red felt-tip?" Josh asked. His ears were a little less red as he took the pin.

"No." Alastair was adamant. "It has to be a blood oath."

Josh took a deep breath and stuck the pin in. He smeared his name across the page with his bloody thumb and put his thumb in his mouth.

"Don't put it in your mouth," Alastair said. "Your mouth is full of germs."

"I always do," Josh said. "It makes it feel better."

Sometimes, Alastair thought, Josh could be such a baby.

He folded up the oath and put it in his secret hiding place where Claudia would never find it. He had hollowed out a square in one of his *Tom Sawyer* books (he had two copies), and kept his treasures and secrets there. At the moment, the only thing in the hollow was a note from Christy, the girl in his class who had black hair so long she could sit on it, and a silver dollar his grandfather had given him.

"I need a Band-Aid," Josh said.

But Alastair didn't want to leave him alone in the room with Spike. Not yet. He glanced at the wastebasket. It wasn't moving.

"My secret is something that you'd never guess. Not in a zillion years."

"All right," Josh said. "I've signed your oath. It better be good."

"It will be." Alastair took the comic book off the top of the wastebasket. He lifted Spike out and set him on the floor beside Josh. "This is my pet dragon, Spike."

Josh had a skeptical look on his face. "It's not real."

Spike moved his foot. Josh smiled. "Big deal. Where's the controller?"

"There's no controller. It's a real, live dragon." Alastair held his hands up in the air.

Just then Spike yawned, showing all his little spiky teeth.

Josh leaped three feet back. His eyes bulged. His ears nearly burst into flame.

"Great galloping gorillas!" he sputtered. "It is real!"

"I told you."

"But it can't be. A dragon, I mean," Josh protested. "There's no such thing except in books."

"That's what I thought, too."

Josh walked around the dragon, looking at it from all angles. "Where did you get it?"

Alastair explained about the petunias and daisies. "I probably should have named him Petunia. If he'd been a girl I would've."

"What are you going to do with him?"

"Keep him," Alastair said with determination. "He's my pet."

"But what can you do with him? I mean, he's a dragon. Don't they eat people?"

"Not this one. He's a vegetarian."

Spike smiled at Josh and walked over to him. Josh edged back toward the door.

"Does he bite?"

"I told you. He's a vegetarian."

"Yeah. But he could still bite."

"He doesn't. At least he's never bitten me." Alastair scritched Spike under his chin. Spike purred. "See, he's tame. Go ahead and pet him."

Josh put out a timid finger. He touched Spike on the head. "Hey, he feels warm. I thought dragon scales would be cold and, well, scaly. These feel like warm satin." He scritched Spike's ears. The little dragon purred and rubbed against him.

"He's just like a cat," Josh said.

"He's sort of like a dog, too. He plays fetch and tug-of-war."

"He's real little. Do you think he will grow?"

"I don't know. Dragon books don't have a lot of technical information. I guess I'll find out."

"He's neat. What did your parents say?"

"They don't know. You know Claudia's allergic to pets. You have to help me keep him a secret from her.

She almost suspected something a while ago. But you fooled her when you kicked the wall. That was quick thinking."

"I thought you had an animal in the trash can," Josh said with a grin, "a frog or a puppy maybe, but I never thought it would be a dragon!"

Chapter Eleven

"The worst thing about having a dragon," Alastair told Josh, "is the bathroom business. I'm getting tired of cleaning out his box. It wouldn't be so bad if I could take him outside."

They were sprawled in the den. They had the run of the house. Claudia and his parents were at the mall picking up the cake for the party and shopping for last-minute items that Claudia said no slumber party would be a slumber party without. Things like rainbow-colored popcorn.

"Why can't you?" Josh asked. "Take him outside, I mean."

"Oh, sure," Alastair said. "Just walk down the street with a dragon on a leash."

"Yeah. I see what you mean. People would go crazy if they saw a real live dragon."

Alastair sat up. "Maybe they wouldn't."

"What are you, crazy? Can you imagine Mr. Hobson if he saw you walking with a dragon?"

"What if he didn't know it was a dragon? What if I disguised Spike?"

"As what? A monkey? You going to rent a monkey suit and tell people he's your new pet monkey?" Josh snorted at his joke.

"Not as a monkey. As a dog."

"How you going to do that? Rent a dog suit?" Josh snickered.

"Don't be silly. Let me think."

Alastair looked at the silvery blue dragon with the pointed tail. Spike was worrying the edge of the sofa.

"He isn't very big," Alastair said. "We could dress him like one of those dogs that look like a mop. All we have to do is tie one of those stringy mopheads on him. Maybe Mom has one. She uses sponge mops, but I'll check."

Alastair couldn't find a string mop but he did find a dust mop. It was a rusty red color and didn't look as though it had been used much. He took it off the handle. He and Josh pinned old shoelaces to the sides. Then they slipped it over Spike and tied the ends under his stomach.

"He doesn't look much like a dog," Alastair said.

"Sure he does," Josh said. "But he needs something on his head."

The boys searched the house. Finally they settled for some orange yarn they found in the sewing box. "I know how to make pom-poms," Alastair said. "Claudia showed me how."

He quickly made a floppy pom-pom and tied it to the dragon's head. He made smaller ones to disguise Spike's tail. For a collar he put a hole in his belt. The rest of the belt was the leash. He could still wear the belt as a belt. Nobody would know the extra hole was there to turn it into a dragon's collar.

"Nobody will ever guess that he's not a dog," Alastair said.

But out on the sidewalk he began to worry. "It would be better to do this at night," he said as he glanced around the neighborhood. He hoped Mr. Hobson wasn't home.

"Yeah, but all those girls will be here then. This is the perfect time. It's too hot to be outside. Everybody is inside watching baseball or gone off to the mall or the pool."

"I guess you're right," Alastair said.

The boys walked slowly along the sidewalk stopping every few seconds for Spike to sniff something.

They had the sidewalk to themselves. Two cars

66

passed in the street but neither driver noticed the dragon at the end of the leash. The boys walked to the end of the block. Spike pooped behind a bush, leaving a neat pile of vegetable-colored droppings.

Things were going really great until they turned around to go back.

As they approached Mr. Hobson's yard, he popped up from behind a hydrangea bush. He had a pair of giant clippers in one hand. The blades were shiny. Alastair bet he wasn't really clipping anything. He was always trying to catch the boys doing something like stepping on his grass or ducking through one of his many hedges or sailing boats on his fish pool. A red-billed cap with green letters that spelled "flower power" shaded his already-pink face from the sun.

"What's that thing you boys are dragging on that leash?" he demanded.

Alastair's instinct told him to run. But Mr. Hobson pinned them with his black eyes.

"This?" Alastair stalled. "This is my new dog."

"New dog, eh? Not very big, is he?"

"No," Alastair replied.

"He's still a puppy," Josh explained.

"He's a funny-looking dog. I've never seen any dogs that look like that. What kind of dog is he?"

"He's a, er . . ." Alastair started to say dragon hound but caught himself in time. He had talked about dragons to Mr. Hobson. He might remember. "He's a teagle," he said quickly.

"Teagle, eh?"

"That's right. Teagle," Alastair said more firmly than he felt.

Mr. Hobson stroked his mustache. "I never heard of any teagle."

"It's a new breed," Josh said.

"New breed, eh?"

"That's right," Alastair said, feeling like a parrot repeating himself. "It's a new breed from China. My Uncle George got him for me. He travels a lot, you know."

Mr. Hobson squinted at Spike from under his hat.

Alastair tugged gently on the leash. "Let's go, boy." To Mr. Hobson he said, "We have to go home now. My mom will be back soon and we have things to do."

"Mind you don't let that dog get in my prize dahlias now. Keep it out of my yard. I plan to win my share of prizes at the flower show this year." He gave the boys a long look. "I'm not going to have a repeat of last year."

The year before, Gruesome had chased a cat across the prize dahlia bed.

"My dog doesn't chase cats," Alastair told Mr. Hobson. "And he's too little to hurt any plants." Alastair didn't say that Spike loved to eat flowers. He would have to keep him away from Mr. Hobson's yard.

"See that he doesn't."

"That wasn't so bad, was it?" Josh asked when they were back in Alastair's room.

"I guess not," Alastair admitted. "But next time I'll do it at night. I don't want to run into Mr. Hobson again in daylight. He was sure looking at Spike hard."

"Do you think he suspected?"

"Yeah. He knows something funny is going on, but he doesn't know what. He'll be watching me even closer now."

Chapter Twelve

The pack of girls arrived for the slumber party promptly at 6:30. Mrs. McKnight gave the boys their instructions. "Stay in Alastair's room except for emergencies."

"What's an emergency?" Josh wanted to know.

"The bathroom. Starvation. Plague. Flood. The usual things," Mrs. McKnight replied.

"It's going to be a long night," Alastair observed as they watched the five girls file in with their sleeping bags.

Besides Claudia there were Bethany, Kirsten, Linda, Kim, and Jennifer. They made a lot of noise as they piled their sleeping bags in the den.

Alastair hoped Spike was tired after his long walk.

He had fed him early, and Spike had curled up for a nap. He was still sleeping at suppertime. Alastair thought it was safe to leave him. The boys were not allowed to eat with the girls. They had to take their hot dogs under the oak tree in the yard while the girls ate in the kitchen. They could hear the giggling all the way outside. There seemed to be a lot of dumb jokes about starfish.

"Why is a starfish like the military?"

"Because it has a lot of arms." More giggles.

Some of the jokes didn't make sense to the boys.

"Why is a starfish like a boy?"

"Because it burps its stomach out."

Shriek, shriek.

"Disgusting," Alastair said.

"Yeah."

As they deposited their paper plates and cups in the kitchen trash, Jennifer yelled, "Starfish alert!" The girls screamed with laughter that followed the boys down the hall to Alastair's room. They closed the door as they had been instructed.

"What a bunch of dopes," Josh said. "I'm glad I don't have an older sister."

Alastair thought Josh's sister Boo was a three-year-old pest, but she was not as bad as Claudia multiplied by five.

"At least they're not right next to us," Alastair said. The girls were sleeping in the den next to the kitchen.

"Yeah. The farther the better."

They settled down to some serious comic book reading. Josh had brought a stack home from camp, and Alastair had new ones his mother had bought to amuse him after the accident. Spike woke up and contented himself chewing Josh's left sneaker. Josh might not have noticed if his foot hadn't been in it. Spike's sharp little teeth punctured Josh's big toe.

"Ye-ouch!" he yelled.

"Quiet. My parents are right down the hall. If we make a lot of noise they'll come down here."

"But Spike bit me!"

"It was an accident. I think he's teething."

"He acts hungry. I thought you fed him."

"I did. But he could be hungry again. He eats a lot," Alastair said.

"In stories dragons only eat once a month or something like that," Josh said. "You know, when the moon was full, they'd go eat a person."

"Those dragons weren't vegetarians. It takes a lot of vegetables and fruit to fill Spike up," Alastair explained.

"Why don't you feed him before he forgets he's a

72

vegetarian and decides to nibble my toes again," Josh suggested.

"I don't have anything. He's eaten all his food. He doesn't usually eat this late. Maybe he's growing."

"Well, get him some more."

"I can't. It's in the kitchen. We're not supposed to go in there," Alastair said.

"Your mom didn't say we couldn't go in the kitchen," Josh argued. "Just the den."

"We're supposed to stay in my room except in an emergency."

"This is an emergency."

There was a loud growl from Spike. The boys looked at him.

"It was his stomach," Alastair said. "He must really be hungry."

"We could go around the other way," Josh suggested.

Spike's stomach growled again, louder this time.

"I guess we'll have to," Alastair said. "We can't listen to his stomach all night. Besides, if it gets louder my parents might hear him. Let's go."

Josh went first. Alastair closed the door behind him but quietly so it wouldn't click. The light was off in the hall except for a night light near the bathroom door. "We'll go single file," Alastair directed. "Follow me. I know where all the creaky boards are." His parents' door was closed. He could hear the low hum of their TV even with the bursts of giggles from the den.

At the end of the hall they tiptoed across the doorway, slithered along the wall, dropped to the floor, and crawled across the living room. But in the dining room Josh bumped into the table. Alastair caught his foot on a chair leg. Something clunked with a metallic twang and something else rang with a crystal vibration. The boys froze.

"What was that?" somebody yelled.

"What?"

"It sounded like an earthquake."

"It was probably a giant starfish trying to get in."

Shriek. Shriek.

The boys waited awhile but nobody came. "Let's go," Alastair said.

They slithered into the kitchen. The refrigerator was on the other side of the room.

"Get some more chips, Kirsten," somebody said.

Alastair and Josh ducked behind the breakfast bar.

Kirsten came in the kitchen and looked in the cabinets. The boys flattened themselves against the bar.

"I don't see any chips."

"Look in the pantry," Claudia said.

Kirsten went into the pantry. When she came out she would be facing Alastair and Josh.

Chapter Thirteen

They were in for it now, Alastair thought as he listened to Kirsten rummaging in the pantry. Alastair pointed to the dining room. Josh nodded.

First Alastair, then Josh zipped across the kitchen floor and into the safety of the dining room.

"What was that?" they heard Kirsten ask.

"What was what?" Claudia said.

"That whooshing sound. Sort of like giant mice."

"It was probably the air conditioning," Claudia said. "Sometimes it makes funny noises when it shifts gears."

The boys grinned.

"That was close," Josh said.

"Giant mice." Alastair snickered.

"Better than giant starfish."

"OK," Alastair said, "let's go."

They sneaked back into the kitchen. Alastair eased open the refrigerator door. He grabbed celery and half a head of lettuce. Josh collected apples and carrots. Then came the hard part. They had to shut the refrigerator door without making noise.

The girls had turned off the lights in the den. Alastair listened for a second.

". . . and then a hand came in the window."

They were telling scary stories. Alastair slid the door shut until it clicked. He and Josh were turning to go back to the living room when the den erupted in screams. The house was filled with them, high screams, low screams, screams in the middle, long continuous screams, short yipping screams.

Alastair didn't wait to find out if they had been caught. "Let's get out of here," he whispered to Josh. They dashed through the darkened rooms and down the hall to Alastair's room.

Alastair stopped short.

"The door is open."

"Who cares? Let's just get in and pretend we've been in bed," Josh said.

"I thought I closed it."

"So what?"

"Where's Spike?" Alastair didn't even look in his room. He raced to the den before his parents could get there. He was afraid of what he was going to see.

The den was empty of girls. They had run into the kitchen and shut the door behind them. Alastair's eyes swept the room. There was stuff all over the place. Sleeping bags covered most of the floor. The small spaces between bags were filled with soda cans, bags of cookies, magazines, hairbrushes, multicolored popcorn, chip bags, and bowls of dip. The room looked as if a hurricane had hit it. In the middle of the mess Alastair found what he was looking for.

Spike was standing in a basket of potato chips, lapping up dip as fast as his curly little tongue could lap.

Alastair didn't stop to think. He scooped up the dragon, stuck him in his sling and sprinted back down to his room just as his parents' door opened.

"What's going on?" he asked as if he had just stepped out of his own room.

"Yeah," Josh said quickly, rubbing his eyes as though he were sleepy.

Mrs. McKnight gave them a sharp look as she tied the sash of her robe.

"You boys wait in your room," Mr. McKnight said.

Alastair waited until his parents had gone into the den. Then he stashed Spike in his shoe box in the closet.

"He was gobbling their dip," he told Josh. "I hope he's full. Maybe he'll go to sleep in there."

The boys put all the dragon food in another box beside Spike's. They kept the apples out in case Alastair's parents had noticed that the boys were carrying food.

"He must have tried to follow us," Alastair said. How could he have left the door ajar? He was so sure it had closed. Maybe it had popped open the way it did sometimes when the latch didn't click. Alastair didn't know what he would do if his parents and Claudia found out about Spike. He couldn't give up his dragon.

"Maybe they didn't notice him with all the screaming," Josh offered.

Alastair thought that sometimes Josh could be so dopey. "What do you think they were screaming at?"

"Well, I sort of thought they were screaming at us," Josh said.

"I thought so, too. But only for a minute. They would have pounced on us. No, they saw him, all right, and we're going to be in trouble. I'll probably have to get rid of Spike."

They sat side by side on the bed and waited. The screaming had stopped. From the den came the excited voices of the girls interspersed with comments from Alastair's parents.

"It had a long forked tail!"

"And a long pointed tongue!"

"And huge teeth!"

"How big was it?" Mr. McKnight asked.

"The size of a German shepherd."

"As big as the sofa."

"It had horrible eyes!"

"They were red!"

"They were green!"

"It was breathing fire!"

"And roaring!"

The voices grew quieter until the boys could only catch a word here and there. At last Alastair's mother came to the door.

"Are you two OK?"

"Sure, Mom. What's going on?"

"The girls were telling horror stories." She smiled. "Their imaginations went a little too far."

Alastair's father came in. "You haven't seen any little green men wandering around, have you?"

"No," Alastair answered truthfully.

"Any potato-chip-eating starfish? Gargoyles wading in dip? Aliens? Monster lizards?"

The boys shook their heads to each question.

"Gavin, you'll give them nightmares," Mrs. McKnight cautioned.

"No, I won't. I think these two are made of sterner stuff. If Alastair saw a dragon, I think he would try to get it to follow him home. Remember when we went to Disney World and he wanted to bring home the baby armadillo he found behind the motel?"

Alastair laughed with his parents but they were uncomfortably close to the truth. "I could've kept it in a terrarium," he defended himself.

"Baby armadillos grow up," said his father. "And I don't think Mr. Hobson would like to have one in the neighborhood. They do a lot of damage in gardens."

"That was a close call," Josh said when Alastair's parents had gone back to bed.

"Yeah."

"We're lucky those goofy girls have so much imagination. Your parents didn't believe they saw anything."

"Yeah," Alastair said again. "We were real lucky."

But Alastair didn't feel lucky. He went to sleep thinking about what his father had said. Baby armadillos grow up.

Maybe baby dragons did, too. Then how would he keep Spike a secret?

Chapter Fourteen

"Do you think he's grown any?" Alastair asked Josh a few days later as they were playing Dinosaurs.

Josh looked at Spike playing with a Ping-Pong ball. He rolled it along the floor with his nose, then gave it a hard swipe with his paw. The ball slammed into the wall, bounced back, and hit Spike on the nose.

"*Yipe yipe yipe!*" The dragon ran behind the bedpost and peered around it at the ball.

"Nope," Josh said. "He still looks the same to me."

"He eats a lot. He ought to be growing."

"Maybe dragons are slow growers," Josh offered.

"If only I knew more about dragons. I wonder why Uncle George hasn't answered my letter."

Alastair decided to keep a record of Spike's growth.

He would measure and weigh him every week. It would be a scientific record.

He bought a new notebook and wrote on the first page DRAGON DATA. He copied his comparison with dragons of old onto the next page. Then he wrote down all the things he had learned about Spike: the food he liked to eat, the food he didn't like, the things he was afraid of, the things he liked to play with. He wrote down things he'd read about dragons in books that he had found to be untrue. Dragons weren't evil. At least his dragon wasn't. His dragon didn't eat people. His dragon didn't fly. It didn't even have wings.

With a measuring tape from his mother's sewing basket, Alastair measured Spike. First he measured length from the tip of his nose to the tip of his tail. Then he measured around the dragon's stomach, the length of his front and back legs, nose to the beginning of his tail, and length of tail. He wrote all the figures down.

Measuring Spike was the easy part. Weighing him wasn't.

Alastair took Spike into the bathroom and carefully locked the door. He didn't want Claudia bursting in on them. She was still suspicious. "I know you were responsible for that monster," she'd told him the day after the slumber party. Alastair swore he was innocent.

He put Spike down beside the scale. Spike tried to run away. Alastair picked him up and put him on it.

Spike jumped around so that his weight didn't register.

Alastair tried putting a bit of carrot, celery, or apple on the scale. Spike knocked each bite off every time with one slap of his tail, then gobbled the food and smiled at Alastair.

"Hey, fella, how am I ever going to keep my record of you if you won't let yourself be weighed?" Alastair asked with exasperation.

There was a knock at the door. "Who's in there with you?" Claudia demanded.

"Nobody."

"Well, hurry up, will you? I'm going to the movie and I've got to wash my hair."

"Use Mom's bathroom."

"I can't. All my stuff is in this one."

"All right. I'll be out in a minute."

Silence.

"Are you still there?" Alastair asked.

"Yes. And I'm going to stay here until you come out. I'm in a hurry, I told you."

"I heard you. Go away and I'll come out."

"No."

Alastair sighed. Claudia could be very stubborn when she thought something was going on that she didn't know about.

"What are you doing in there, anyway?"

"Nothing."

"Then come out and do nothing in your room."

She was never going to leave. He would have to sneak Spike past her in his sling.

"I'm weighing myself."

He picked up the dragon and put him in the sling. Then he stepped noisily on the scale. The scale registered sixty-four pounds.

Alastair looked down at the number in surprise. He'd never weighed that much before. He put the dragon on the floor and checked his weight on the scale again. Sixty pounds. So Spike weighed four pounds. Alastair wrote that in his notebook.

He picked Spike up and stuffed him in his sling again. He threw a big bath towel over his right shoulder so that it covered his hand in case Spike poked his nose out of the sling. Then he unlocked the bathroom door and took Spike out right under Claudia's nosy nose. All she saw was the notebook Alastair was carrying.

But not because she wasn't looking. Alastair didn't know if she was being her usual suspicious self or if she had any real evidence. He'd been so careful to hide all traces of his dragon.

Chapter Fifteen

During the first two weeks of Alastair's record-keeping, Spike's weight didn't change. Alastair was beginning to worry that Spike wasn't getting enough to eat.

"He eats all the time," Josh pointed out, "except when he's asleep or playing. He looks healthy to me."

"How many dragons have you seen?"

"None. But I know about cats. As long as Elton eats well, sleeps, and plays, he's OK. Except for hair balls."

"How do you know when he's sick?"

"I don't know. I don't think he's ever sick. But my mom once said you feel a dog's nose to see if it's sick. She says if it's hot and dry, it means he's sick."

Alastair felt Spike's nose.

"It feels warm and dry to me."

"*Yup,*" Spike chirped.

"You check it," he told Josh.

Josh touched the dragon's nose. "It does feel a little bit warm. But he doesn't act sick. Maybe dragons' noses are supposed to be dry and warm."

The third week when Alastair subtracted his weight from the weight of himself and the dragon, Spike had gained almost half a pound.

"I guess you're not sick, little fella." He scritched Spike under the chin.

"*Djeeeeep,*" Spike purred.

But it was the letter from Uncle George that excited Alastair. At last he would find out all he needed to know about dragons.

> *Dear Alastair,*
>
> *I apologize for not writing sooner, but I was in Chile checking out a lake monster rumor. I was sorry to hear about your accident. I don't suppose your dad told you about the time I broke my arm trying to fly off the garage in a cape made from an old towel.*
>
> *No, he wouldn't. It was his idea. But he had a suspicion that it might not work. He had never seen people flying around all over the place in their towels. So he told his little brother how much fun it would be, and I ended up with the broken*

arm and had to miss all the fun of summer.

Meantime, I don't have much information about modern dragons. There is a lot of superstition about them, but most of it is worthless. For instance, dragons eating young women. The institute believes that these stories are rooted in the shame a family felt when a daughter ran off with an unsuitable young man. The dragon was a convenient scapegoat to save face in the village. And there are others.

We would like to have a documented sighting of a dragon. If you want to read about monster sightings that are not documented, there is the Loch Ness monster in Scotland, Nessie it's called. The Great Lakes have a monster, New Jersey has one, South Carolina has the lizard man, Oregon has Bigfoot. The institute keeps a record of all these sightings. Some of them might be real just as some are a result of overimagination, wishful thinking, hysteria, or a desire for media attention. But we believe that there is a basis for these sightings.

Let me know if you sight a dragon. I've always wanted to see one.

Keep in touch.

Love,
Uncle George

Alastair decided to send a picture of Spike to his uncle.

"He'll keep my secret," he told Josh.

"But how?" Josh asked. "You don't have a camera. And anyway if you take the film to be developed, the developers will see it and your secret will be out."

"I should have pictures of Spike for my scientific record," Alastair insisted. "I'll figure out a way."

"There might be a way," Josh said. "I mean, I might be able to help you take one picture."

"How can I take just one?"

"My dad has a Polaroid. You could take one to send to your uncle. But only one because my dad will notice if we take any more."

"One is better than none," Alastair said.

Josh ran home for the camera. He brought it back in his backpack. "We have to be careful with it."

"Can we take it inside?"

"Sure. It has a flash."

Alastair decided to sit beside Spike and hold a measuring tape to show his size. "That's the scientific way to do it," he told Josh.

Josh pressed the button. The camera went into action. First it flashed a bright light. Then it whirred and made all sorts of noises.

"*Yeeeeeeeeppppp,*" Spike yelled.

He ran under Alastair's bed, but not all the way. His

back legs and tail stuck out. The boys laughed.

"I wish we could get a picture of that," Alastair said as he hauled the quivering little dragon out and comforted him.

"It's all right, Spike. It's OK, little fella. It's all over. It's not going to hurt you."

"Syup syup syup," sniffled the dragon.

Alastair sent the picture to his uncle. Then he wrote a letter. He told Uncle George how he had found Spike in the daisy bed. He copied all the dragon data he'd recorded on Spike. This was real documented evidence.

Chapter Sixteen

Every night since they'd thought up the dog suit Alastair dressed Spike in it after supper and took him out for a walk. His parents and Claudia were always busy then. Josh came over to go with him in case of trouble.

For several weeks they managed to avoid Mr. Hobson. The boys had watched him for a few days. When he wasn't away at work Mr. Hobson puttered in his yard, mowing, weeding, trimming, fertilizing late in the afternoons. But at about six he always went back in his house and stayed for over half an hour before he came back out to putter again. This was the time the boys walked Spike.

A week after Alastair had written to Uncle George, the boys got ready for their walk. It was easy getting

Spike out. Claudia was in the bathroom taking her usual hour-long bubble bath. Mrs. McKnight was watching the news in the den. Mr. McKnight was in the bedroom watching a baseball game. The sidewalk was clear. Most people were at home eating.

"Spike has gained another quarter of a pound," Alastair said. "I don't know what I'll do when he outgrows his dog suit."

"You could buy him another mop," Josh said. "Or maybe get one of those little doggy raincoats. You could cut the mop in two pieces and sew one on each side of the raincoat. My neighbor Mrs. McKeithen has a Scottie. He wears a cute little plaid raincoat when it's raining."

"How much do they cost?" Alastair was asking when he saw Gruesome galloping out of nowhere straight at them.

Alastair froze. He had forgotten about Gruesome. The Whipples had been on vacation and Gruesome had been boarded at a farm. "Oh no," he wailed. "Gruesome hates cats! He'll think Spike is a cat and try to kill him."

Gruesome's mouth was open. It was full of huge teeth. His tongue was big and rubbery and dripping with slobber. It looked as though it could snap Spike up in one gulp. Gruesome galloped faster as his eyes caught sight of Spike.

"No, Gruesome, no!" the boys shouted. But the dog kept coming.

"Quick! Over here," Josh said urgently as he headed for the nearest tree.

But Spike wouldn't budge. He stood his ground and Alastair stayed with him.

"No, Gruesome, no! Come on, Spike, hurry!" Alastair shouted but neither Spike nor Gruesome paid attention to him. He bent to pick Spike up but the little dragon hopped out of his reach.

Gruesome was only three feet away. His mouth hung open. Alastair could almost feel the dog's hot breath. But Spike still wouldn't run. The dragon took a huge breath and puffed himself up to twice his normal size. Now he was bigger than a cat. He bulged out of the dog suit. Parts of it hung on by its strings. Spike let out a loud roar.

Gruesome skidded to a stop but it was too late.

Spike opened his mouth again, and this time out came a spurt of flame.

It shot out three feet and singed Gruesome's nose. The dog sniffed the air as he tried to look cross-eyed at his nose. Then he seemed to realize what had happened. He whimpered once and took off across the grass.

Spike jerked the leash out of Alastair's hand and tore out after the dog. Alastair stared in amazement.

"Wow!" Josh said. "Look at that dragon go!"

"Don't stand there like a telephone pole," Alastair said as he raced after Spike. "Help me catch him. They're headed for Mr. Hobson's house."

Spike had never run away before. Alastair had never even seen him run. Up to now the most movement he'd seen in Spike was in his games of fetch and tug-of-war.

But now the dragon was a streak of silvery blue as he tore along the sidewalk behind Gruesome. When they reached Mr. Hobson's yard, Gruesome scrambled under the hedge and swerved across the velvety lawn with Spike right behind him.

Alastair ran after them. Josh was right behind him. When they reached the backyard, Gruesome was cooling his nose in the fish pool.

Spike was racing straight toward Gruesome. The dog looked up and saw Spike. He yelped once and jumped over the pool. He landed with all four feet running.

Spike had to go around the pool. He was almost on the other side when Mr. Hobson came outside. "Hey!" he yelled. "What's going on out here?"

Gruesome ran through the flower beds.

"Oh no!" Alastair groaned, "not the flowers."

Gruesome went through the roses first. Spike stopped abruptly and sampled a red rose, then a pink one. Then he cleaned the orange roses off a bush. Gruesome made his escape while the dragon was munching a yellow rose.

"Get out of there you vicious dog! Get out of my prize roses!" Mr. Hobson bellowed.

But the more he yelled, the more Spike ate. He pulled the tall roses down with his paws, eating them like sandwiches.

Mr. Hobson picked up a hoe by his back door. He ran with great galloping steps over to the rose bed, whacking all the while with the hoe. Spike gobbled faster.

"He's going to kill Spike!" Josh gasped.

"We've got to stop him. Spike!" Alastair cried, giving himself away to Mr. Hobson.

But Mr. Hobson ignored Alastair. "I've got you now!" he crowed at Spike.

The dragon looked up at Mr. Hobson bearing down on him with the hoe. He started to puff himself up.

"No, Spike. No!" Alastair shouted. He couldn't let Spike incinerate Mr. Hobson.

Spike hesitated a fraction of a second. Then with a burst of speed he dodged Mr. Hobson's hoe and ran through his legs and into the hollyhocks with Mr. Hobson behind him slashing right and left with the hoe.

Alastair and Josh followed the trail of the fallen hollyhocks. Spike ran into the dahlia bed.

"Not the dahlias!" Alastair panted, remembering the flower show.

But Mr. Hobson didn't seem to remember. He

hacked the dahlias worse than he had the hollyhocks. Spike raced through the dahlias, stopping only once to bite off a luscious purple-petaled one, which he nibbled on the run.

Then he doubled back between Mr. Hobson's feet and ran straight to Alastair. He was still chewing when Alastair picked him up. Mr. Hobson seemed to see Alastair for the first time.

"I might have known that dratted dog of yours would wreck my flowers," he yelled. His face was as purple as the petals of the dahlia hanging from Spike's mouth.

Alastair and Josh didn't wait to hear what Mr. Hobson was yelling. They crashed through the shrubbery and climbed the fence into Alastair's backyard. They didn't stop until they were in Alastair's room.

The boys collapsed on the floor. A few minutes later Alastair heard the phone ring.

"Oh boy. We're in trouble now," Alastair said. He sat up and looked at the dragon. "Why did you do it, fella?"

Spike looked at him with round innocent eyes as he finished the last of the dahlia.

"Everything was going just great," Alastair went on. "Now I'm going to lose the only real pet I ever had."

"You had a turtle once," Josh corrected him. "Its name was Trudy. I remember Claudia shut the car doo—"

95

"Oh, shut up," Alastair interrupted. "A turtle isn't a real pet. Not like a dragon. Spike is the best pet in the world. Nobody else in the whole world has a dragon."

"He may not be the best pet, but he's certainly the only dragon pet," Josh said.

Alastair didn't argue. He hugged Spike as he waited for Mr. Hobson to tell his parents.

Chapter Seventeen

Alastair didn't have long to wait. A few minutes later he heard his parents go out.

"Well, I think I'll go home now," Josh said as he got up.

"Mr. Hobson saw you, too," Alastair reminded him. Josh sat back down.

The McKnights came back. "Alastair, Josh, will you come in here, please," Mrs. McKnight called from the living room.

The boys trudged as slowly as possible into the living room. Mr. Hobson was there, still holding on to his hoe. His face had paled to puce. He'd lost his hat, and the top of his bald head was puce, too. Alastair wanted to giggle. He didn't dare look at Josh.

"Alastair," his father began, "Mr. Hobson says your dog tore up his prize flower beds, ate his roses, and ruined his chances at the flower show this week. I told him you didn't have a dog. This is true, isn't it? You're not hiding a dog, are you?"

All eyes turned to Alastair. It was up to him. What could he say that would save his dragon and still be the truth?

"No, Dad. I'm not hiding a dog."

"I saw you," Mr. Hobson shouted.

"Don't shout, Leonard," Mrs. McKnight said.

"What did all that damage out there if it wasn't that dog of yours?" Mr. Hobson demanded as he gestured with his hoe.

"Careful," Mr. McKnight cautioned as the hoe just missed a lamp.

"I don't have a dog," Alastair said. "And most of the damage was done by Mr. Hobson with his hoe. He ruined his own dahlias and hollyhocks."

"Why, that . . ." Mr. Hobson sputtered.

"Is that the truth, Alastair?" asked his father.

"Yes, Dad. It's the honest truth." Alastair met his father's eyes.

"What about that teagle I saw you with," Mr. Hobson said.

"I was only walking it," Alastair said. "It wasn't my dog."

98

"But you were in Mr. Hobson's yard tonight?" his father said.

"Yes, sir."

"Then I think it's only fair that you and Josh go over tomorrow and help Mr. Hobson repair some of the damage to his yard. Is that good enough for you, Leonard?"

"It won't bring my dahlias back," Mr. Hobson growled. "That dog ate my whole summer."

"If the flower show is tomorrow, you should pick them tonight anyway, shouldn't you?" Mrs. McKnight spoke up. "Maybe some of them aren't too damaged by the hoe." She glanced at the weapon. "Maybe you could salvage some of them to enter tomorrow."

Mr. Hobson didn't wait to reply. He turned and hurried out the door.

"Now, Alastair, let's see this teagle of yours," his father said.

Chapter Eighteen

Alastair looked at his father. How did he know?

"OK, Dad. I'll get him."

"Wait here, Josh," Mr. McKnight said as Josh started to follow Alastair to his room.

Alastair found Spike curled up asleep under his bed. He straightened the dog suit and scritched Spike's ears.

"You shouldn't have done it, Spike," he told the dragon. "Now they're going to make me get rid of you because of Claudia's allergies."

The dragon purred and arched his back. He butted his head against Alastair's hand to make him scritch some more.

Alastair put his face down against the dragon's. "Maybe whoever takes you will let me visit you sometimes." A tear dropped out of the corner of his eye and trickled down Spike's nose. Alastair sniffed back the other tears.

"Come on, little fella." He picked up his dragon. "I guess we can't put it off any longer."

He went back to the living room, where his family and Josh were waiting.

"Here he is," he said. "Here's the teagle that tore up Mr. Hobson's yard." He put Spike down in the middle of the floor.

"My allergies!" Claudia shrieked. "I can feel them starting. I'm going to sneeze."

"Don't be silly," Alastair told her. "Spike has been here all summer. You're just pretending."

Claudia made loud sniffing noises, but no sneezes came.

His mother looked interested. "All summer?"

"Since the Tuesday after my accident. It was Spike who ate the petunias."

"That certainly is the funniest dog I've ever seen," his father said.

"He really isn't a dog," Josh spoke up eagerly.

Alastair gave him a look that meant you-swore-an-oath-not-to-tell.

"I was only trying to help," Josh said. "They're going to find out anyway."

"Find out what?" his parents asked in one voice.

"That he isn't a dog," Alastair said.

"I think we can ascertain that," said his father. "But just what is he? There's no such animal as a teagle."

"He's a dragon," Alastair said in a low voice.

"A what?" said Claudia and his parents together.

"He's a dragon!" Josh piped up.

"Oh, come on." Claudia looked disgusted as she tried again to summon up a sneeze.

"He really is," Josh said eagerly. "Show them, Alastair."

Alastair took the dog suit off Spike, who was revealed in all his dragonness.

No one spoke.

Finally his father said in a funny tone, "I think I'll call George."

"Call George what?" said a voice from the front door.

"It's Uncle George!" Claudia said. "Did you bring me any earrings?"

"Claudia, that's no way to greet your uncle," said her mother.

"He promised to bring me some exotic earrings on his next trip," Claudia explained.

But Uncle George didn't hear her. His attention was riveted on the little dragon in the middle of the floor.

"Well," he said, "this is real documented evidence, Alastair."

Alastair nodded.

"How do you know that?" Alastair's father asked.

"Alastair wrote me all about his dragon," Uncle George explained. "I came as soon as I got his letter. He knew I'd be fascinated."

"But, Alastair, where did you *get* this creature?" his mother asked.

Alastair told them about the petunias and the daisies.

"But that still doesn't explain where it came from," she said.

"And why did you dress him in the dog suit?" Claudia asked.

"I had to take him outside so I wouldn't have to clean up his dragon poop," Alastair said. "I couldn't walk him looking like a dragon. So I disguised him as a dog."

"Clever," said his father.

"More than clever, Gavin," Uncle George said, "ingenious."

"I'm surprised Leonard was taken in," said Mr. McKnight. He laughed. "Teagle, indeed. I can't wait to see his face when I tell him the truth. He was purple tonight. I wonder what color he'll be then."

"I don't think we want to do that, Gavin," said Uncle George. "You'll be overrun with media people, sightseers, hucksters, even kidnappers. Or dragonnappers."

"You're right. I hadn't thought of that," said his

brother. "But you'll be taking the dragon back to the institute with you, won't you? The institute will want to study him."

"This is certainly the breakthrough we've been looking for," Uncle George said.

Alastair felt his stomach turn over.

"Yes," said his mother. "That would be best."

"No, it wouldn't," said Alastair.

"Uncle George will take very good care of the dragon," said his father.

"No," Alastair cried. "He's my pet. You never let me have a pet before because Claudia was allergic. Now I have one she isn't allergic to and you won't let me keep it. It's not fair."

"This dragon is too important for you to keep, Alastair," his father said. "He needs to be studied intensively and scientifically."

"I shouldn't have told you about him," Alastair said to his uncle. "I never thought you'd try to take him away."

"But, Alastair, we can't possibly keep a dragon here . . ." his mother began.

"I don't see why not," Uncle George said. "He's been here all summer."

"I don't know," said his mother. "A dragon. Whoever heard of such a thing?"

"But this is of major importance to natural science,"

Mr. McKnight argued. "Scientists all over the world will want to study this, er, Spike. We can't keep him here in our home."

"It's of major importance to Alastair, too," said Uncle George. "Alastair has been keeping excellent records on the dragon. He sent me a copy. In fact, that is what made me realize that the dragon was real. The picture was good," he said to Alastair, "but people have been known to fake photographs. There was a famous hoax around the turn of the century with paper-doll fairies that two little girls perpetrated with a box camera. And people are always faking pictures of lake monsters. But your records were highly scientific. I vote that Spike be allowed to stay with Alastair. I can check on him from time to time. There are tests that I will conduct. Alastair and Spike can come to the institute for these. How about it, Gavin? Margaret?"

Alastair's father looked at the dragon, then at Alastair. "I don't know," he said.

"Please, Mom, Dad." Alastair felt tears starting. He tried to blink them away but there were too many.

"It seems to me that Alastair has been learning something from this dragon," his mother said.

Everyone looked at her. "He's been learning to think ahead," she continued. "He had to, to conceal the animal, if that's what it is, from his whole family and feed and care for it all these weeks. He even created a dog suit so that he could walk him." She smiled.

Everyone looked at the remains of the dog suit.

"Perhaps we should have a discussion," Uncle George said, looking at Alastair's father.

"I could use a cup of coffee," Mr. McKnight said.

The three adults went to the kitchen.

Alastair strained his ears, but he couldn't hear their voices—only the clink of a spoon against a dish. Spike went over to sniff Claudia's foot. She snatched it away and tucked both feet under her on the chair.

"He doesn't bite," Josh offered.

"He's slimy," she said.

"No, he's really not," Josh said.

It would have worked, Alastair thought, if Gruesome hadn't come along. But he didn't say it. He should have allowed for emergencies like Gruesome or some other dog. But he couldn't have known about Spike's firepower. Alastair kept quiet about that.

Claudia reached out with a cautious finger and stroked Spike's head. He purred and rolled over, waving his paws in the air. "He's kinda cute," she said, "in a reptilian way."

There was a scraping sound from the kitchen as a chair was pushed back. "They're coming back," Josh reported.

Alastair's stomach clenched.

His parents, followed by Uncle George, came back

into the living room. His father cleared his throat. "A dragon is a great responsibility," he began.

Alastair's heart sank to his toes. Tears spilled out of the corners of his eyes. The room had a glassy look.

"You will have a lot to do," his father continued. "You will have to let George teach you what he can but it will be a learning situation for both of you."

"Does that mean I can keep him?" Alastair looked from one parent to the other.

"He is your dragon," his father said.

His mother nodded. "But you have to keep Spike a secret."

"I can do that," Alastair said. He wiped his eyes on his sleeves. "Josh can, too. Can't you, Josh?"

"Sure."

Spike rubbed against Alastair and purred loudly.

"Look! He's acting just like a cat," Claudia said.

"His name is Spike," Alastair told her.

"He's adorable," said Mrs. McKnight. "And Claudia doesn't seem to be at all allergic."

"Djup," said Spike.

"I want to get a recording of that," said Uncle George. "I have some equipment in my van that I'll leave for Alastair. A Polaroid camera, a Camcorder, things like that."

"Oh boy!" Josh said.

"Scientific equipment," Uncle George reminded him.

"Where on earth did the little thing come from?" Mrs. McKnight asked again.

"Probably from somewhere in the earth," said Uncle George. "The institute has been on the track of a Chinese dragon for years, but the closest we've ever come to anything like this in America is the lizard man in South Carolina and a few monsters in the Great Lakes. Man has long believed in the existence of dragons through the myths that have been handed down. Now we have proof that these myths were based on reality. It is possible that this dragon came over long ago on the land bridge from Asia to Alaska and somehow migrated undetected for hundreds of years until it reached the east coast. This one must have been underground somewhere nearby. The road workers may have disturbed it with their jackhammers and their backhoes."

"Do you mean there may be others?" Alastair asked.

"This one certainly had parents at some time," Uncle George said. "But it is difficult to tell when. The egg could have incubated for a long time."

"What does that mean?" Josh asked.

"The time it takes it to hatch," Alastair said.

"That's right," Uncle George said. "The question is how long did it take? Who knows the incubation period of a dragon egg. It could have been hundreds of years if the egg were properly protected from the elements in a cave, perhaps. This one must have been disturbed by

108

something to make it wander into an urban area."

"He was lucky that he wandered into the petunias," Alastair said, "and not into traffic."

"He's certainly kept Alastair occupied all summer while he recuperated from his accident," Mrs. McKnight said. "And I was worried about his being bored!"

"Mr. Hobson was wrong," said Mr. McKnight. "Spike isn't the teagle that ate summer. He's the dragon that ate summer."

"He certainly ate Mr. Hobson's summer," said Uncle George with a laugh. "You boys have a lot of work ahead of you to make up for the wreckage of his garden."

"We'll do it," Alastair promised.

"What about Leonard?" Mrs. McKnight asked. "He saw the dragon."

"He was so upset over his dahlias that he isn't sure what he saw," Mr. McKnight said. "But you boys will have to make sure that you walk Spike away from Mr. Hobson's house."

Later, when he and Josh were alone in his room with Spike, Josh said, "What about the flame? You didn't tell them what Spike almost did to Gruesome and to Mr. Hobson."

"He only did it because he was afraid. He was trying to protect himself," Alastair said. "And he stopped when I told him to. He won't do it again. I can train him. He listens to me."

"Yeah. He does," Josh said. "He's probably a lot like a dog. You can teach him things."

As Alastair watched, Spike pushed a little red car across the room with his nose. "He's very smart," Alastair said. "The best and smartest dragon in the world."

Alastair remembered something he had read about Asian dragons. If Spike's ancestors had come across the land bridge to America, that meant he was an Asian dragon. Asian dragons were good dragons. They were guardian dragons, protective of whatever they were guarding. And they went where they were needed. Spike came to Alastair because he was needed. Now Spike needed him for protection.

"I'll take care of you, little fella," he whispered.

Spike stopped pushing the truck and smiled at Alastair. *"Zheep,"* he purred.

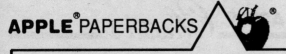

APPLE Classics

❏ MA43389-X	**The Adventures of Huckleberry Finn** Mark Twain	**$2.95**
❏ MA43352-0	**The Adventures of Tom Sawyer** Mark Twain	**$2.95**
❏ MA42035-6	**Alice in Wonderland** Lewis Carroll	**$2.95**
❏ MA44556-1	**Anne of Avonlea** L.M. Montgomery	**$3.25**
❏ MA42243-X	**Anne of Green Gables** L.M. Montgomery	**$2.95**
❏ MA43053-X	**Around the World in Eighty Days** Jules Verne	**$2.95**
❏ MA42354-1	**Black Beauty** Anna Sewell	**$3.25**
❏ MA44001-2	**The Call of the Wild** Jack London	**$2.95**
❏ MA43527-2	**A Christmas Carol** Charles Dickens	**$2.75**
❏ MA45169-3	**Dr. Jekyll & Mr. Hyde: And Other Stories of the Supernatural** Robert Louis Stevenson	**$3.25**
❏ MA42046-1	**Heidi** Johanna Spyri	**$3.25**
❏ MA44016-0	**The Invisible Man** H.G. Wells	**$2.95**
❏ MA40719-8	**A Little Princess** Frances Hodgson Burnett	**$3.25**
❏ MA41279-5	**Little Men** Louisa May Alcott	**$3.25**
❏ MA43797-6	**Little Women** Louisa May Alcott	**$3.25**
❏ MA44769-6	**Pollyanna** Eleanor H. Porter	**$2.95**
❏ MA41343-0	**Rebecca of Sunnybrook Farm** Kate Douglas Wiggin	**$3.25**
❏ MA45441-2	**Robin Hood of Sherwood Forest** Ann McGovern	**$2.95**
❏ MA43285-0	**Robinson Crusoe** Daniel Defoe	**$3.50**
❏ MA42323-1	**Sara Crewe** Frances Hodgson Burnett	**$2.75**
❏ MA43346-6	**The Secret Garden** Frances Hodgson Burnett	**$2.95**
❏ MA44014-4	**The Swiss Family Robinson** Johann Wyss	**$3.25**
❏ MA42591-9	**White Fang** Jack London	**$3.25**
❏ MA44774-2	**The Wind in the Willows** Kenneth Grahame	**$2.95**
❏ MA44089-6	**The Wizard of Oz** L. Frank Baum	**$2.95**

Available wherever you buy books, or use this order form.

Scholastic Inc., P.O. Box 7502, 2931 East McCarty Street, Jefferson City, MO 65102

Please send me the books I have checked above. I am enclosing $ _____ (please add $2.00 to cover shipping and handling). Send check or money order — no cash or C.O.D.s please.

Name _____

Address _____

City _____ State/Zip _____

Please allow four to six weeks for delivery. Available in the U.S. only. Sorry, mail orders are not available to residents of Canada. Prices subject to change.

AC1092